I JUST FORGOT

BY
MERCER MAYER

A GOLDEN BOOK • NEW YORK

Western Publishing Company, Inc., Racine, Wisconsin 53404

For Benjamin

Sometimes I remember, and sometimes I just forget.

This morning I remembered to brush my teeth,
but I forgot to make my bed.

I put my dishes in the sink after breakfast,
but I forgot to put the milk away.

GOOD
MILK

I almost forgot to feed the puppy, but he reminded me.

Grrrr

I didn't forget to water the plants. They looked fine to me.

I didn't forget to feed the goldfish.
He just didn't look hungry. I'll
do it now, Mom.

I got ready for school.
I even got to the school bus on time.

But I forgot my lunch box.

Mom brought it to school for me.
Thanks, Mom.

After school, I went outside to play in the rain.
I remembered to put on my rain slicker.

But I forgot my rubber boots.

When I came inside for a snack, I didn't
forget to take my boots off. I left them
on because I was going right back outside.

I had cookies and milk.

I was just going to eat three cookies, but
I forgot to count them.

I didn't forget to shut the refrigerator door, though.
I just wasn't finished eating yet.

When Dad came home from work, I was supposed to get his paper. I didn't forget—the puppy got it first.

I know it's time for bed. I didn't forget.

Of course I'll remember to pick up my toys when
I'm finished playing with them.

I took my bath and remembered to wash behind my ears.

I didn't use soap, but I didn't forget to. I just don't like soap.

I guess I did forget to pick up my toys.

Did I forget to turn off the tub, too?

But there is one thing I never forget.

I always remember to have Mom
read me a bedtime story. And I always remember
to kiss her good night.